Monster Manners

Hazel Hutchins
illustrated by **Sampar**

Scholastic Canada Ltd.
Toronto New York London Auckland Sydney
Mexico City New Delhi Hong Kong Buenos Aires

If you are ever invited to a
monster's house for dinner,
be sure to mind your manners.

2

Always wash your
hands before coming
to the table,
or the slobber plant
will drool on you.

Always set your
napkin neatly on
your lap,

or it could
pull too
tightly
around
your neck.

Never put your elbows
on the table,
or the table might not
let go afterward.

Always pass dishes in a circle instead of reaching, or a snapping turtle may beat you to it.

Be sure to use your
knife and fork,
or they might find
something else to do.

Always chew with your mouth closed, or the flies will clean your teeth between courses.

Never feed the family pet,
or it could set the house
on fire.

Do not sing, burp loudly
or tell rude jokes,
or the neighbours might
want to join you.

And when everyone at the table is finished eating, be sure to say, "Thank you for a very nice meal. May I be excused to go outside?"

21

Because messy desserts
are always served outside.
And messy desserts are
the best desserts of all.

Scholastic Canada Ltd.
604 King Street West, Toronto, Ontario M5V 1E1, Canada

Scholastic Inc.
557 Broadway, New York, NY 10012, USA

Scholastic Australia Pty Limited
PO Box 579, Gosford, NSW 2250, Australia

Scholastic New Zealand Limited
Private Bag 94407, Botany, Manukau 2163, New Zealand

Scholastic Children's Books
Euston House, 24 Eversholt Street, London NW1 1DB, UK

In this book, the illustrations are done in ink, with a pen and a brush, then scanned and digitally coloured.

Library and Archives Canada Cataloguing in Publication
Hutchins, H. J. (Hazel J.)
      Monster manners / H.J. Hutchins ; illustrated by Sampar.
ISBN 978-1-4431-0015-1
I. Sampar II. Title.
PS8565.U826M66 2011   jC813'.54   C2010-906026-1

6 5 4 3 2 1   Printed in Canada   119   11 12 13 14 15

Mixed Sources
Product group from well-managed
forests, controlled sources and
recycled wood or fiber
www.fsc.org Cert no. SGS-COC-003098
© 1996 Forest Stewardship Council
FSC